THE CARD IN BACK.

A Chocolate Moose

for Dinner

written and illustrated by

FRED GWYNNE

Simon and Schuster Books for Young Readers
Published by Simon & Schuster Inc., New York

Published by Simon and Schuster Books for Young Readers
A Division of Simon & Schuster, Inc.
Simon & Schuster Building
Rockefeller Center
1230 Avenue of the Americas
New York, NY 10020

Originally published by Windmill Books, Inc. and Wanderer Books
Simon and Schuster Books for Young Readers
is a trademark of
Simon & Schuster, Inc.

Designed by Dorothea von Elbe
Manufactured in the United States of America

10 9 8 7 6 5 4 3 2

10 9 8 7 6 5 4 3   pbk

Library of Congress Cataloging in Publication Data
Gwynne, Fred.
    A chocolate moose for dinner.
    SUMMARY: A little girl pictures the things her
parents talk about, such as a chocolate moose,
a gorilla war, and shoe trees.
    1. English language—Homonyms—Juvenile
literature. [1. English language—Homonyms.
2. English language—Terms and phrases] I. Title
PE1595.G73 1980   428.1   80-14150
ISBN 0-671-66685-1
ISBN 0-671-66741-6 (pbk.)

For Keiron, Gaynor, Madyn, Evan, and Furlaud

Mommy says she had a chocolate moose for dinner last night.

And after dinner

she toasted Daddy.

there's a gorilla war.

Daddy says he has trees for all his shoes.

Daddy says lions pray on

other animals.

Daddy says he hates

the arms race.

Mommy says we need a new wing on the house, but Daddy says he'll have to sleep on it.

Daddy says there should

Mommy says her

favorite painter is Dolly.

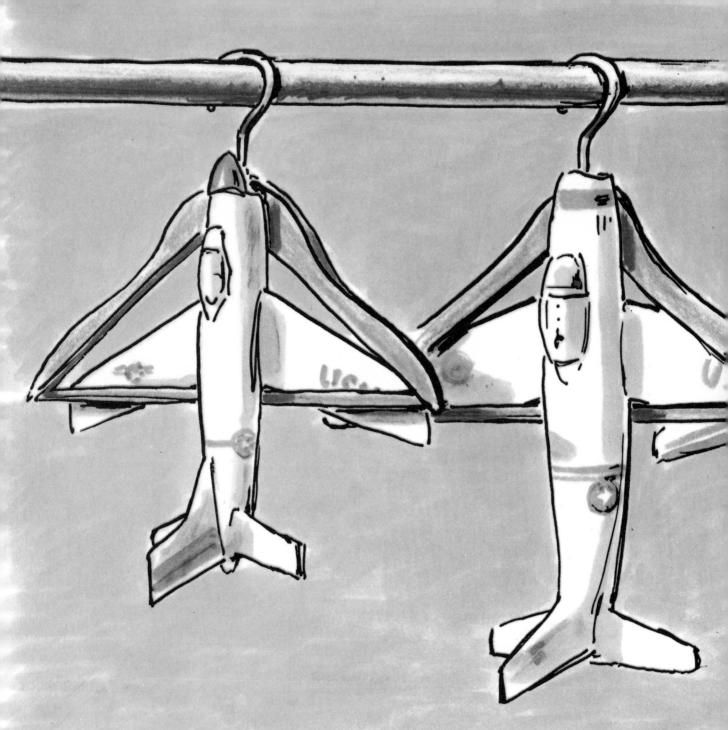

**Mommy says
there are airplane hangers.**

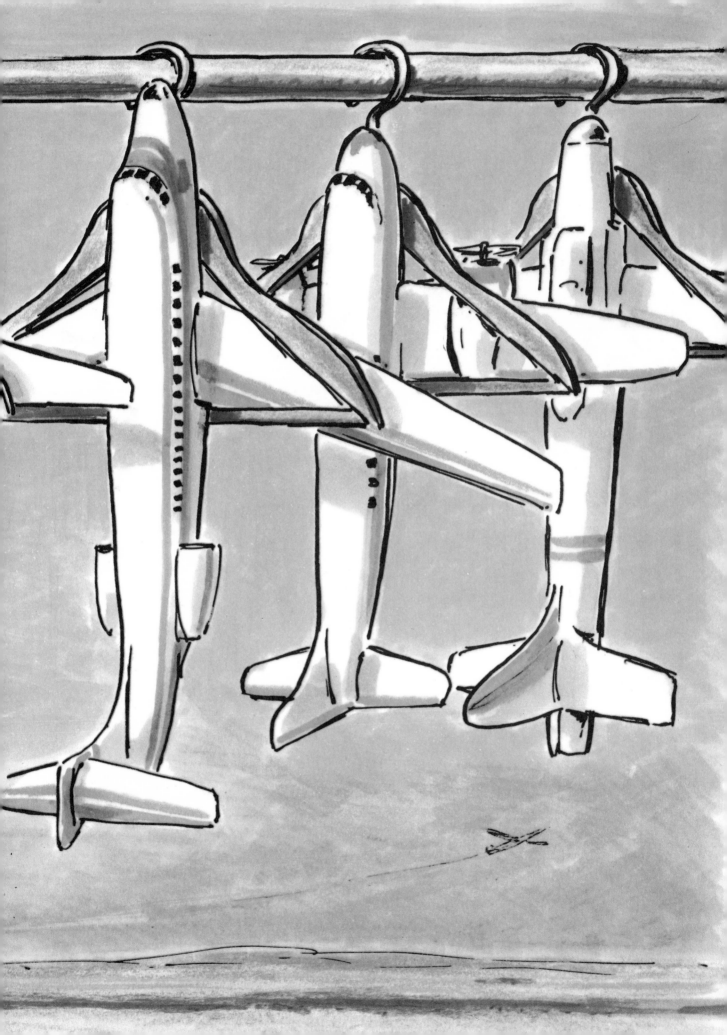

**Daddy says
he has the best
fishing tackle.**

It says on TV a man held up a bank.

He spent two years in the pen.

And he has just escaped and is now on the lamb.

At the ocean Daddy says

Daddy says he plays the piano by ear.

Daddy says that in college

people row in shells.

**And some row
in a single skull.**

Mommy says after she and Daddy argue they always kiss and make up.

Mommy says she's going to tell me about Santa Claws.

And Daddy says he's going to tell me the story of

the tortoise and the hair.

Stories like these drive me up a wall!